The Pinchers and the Diamond Heist

Anders Sparring & Per Gustavsson

THE PINCHERS
and the Diamond Heist

Translated by Julia Marshall

GECKO PRESS

This edition first published in 2024 by Gecko Press
PO Box 9335, Wellington 6141, Aotearoa New Zealand
office@geckopress.com

Familjen Knyckertz och gulddiamanten © Anders Sparring (text),
Per Gustavsson (illustrations), and Natur & Kultur, Stockholm 2018
English edition published in agreement with Koja Agency

Gecko Press aims to publish with a low environmental impact.
Our books are printed using vegetable inks on FSC-certified paper from
sustainably managed forests. We produce books of high quality with
sewn bindings and beautiful paper—made to be read over and over.

The cost of this translation was supported by a subsidy
from the Swedish Arts Council, gratefully acknowledged.

Original language: Swedish
Edited by Penelope Todd
Cover design by Astred Hicks
Design and typesetting by Katrina Duncan
Printed in China by Everbest Printing Co. Ltd,
an accredited ISO 14001 & FSC-certified printer

ISBN hardback: 9781776575664
ISBN paperback: 9781776575671
Ebook available

For more curiously good books, visit geckopress.com

Meet the Pinchers

Rob Pincher

Job: Thief

Tools: Crowbar, dynamite ("The more people can see where you've been, the better.")

Loves to steal: The man next door's newspaper, safes, Theo's socks

Motto: "If you just give a child enough love, the thief (in them) will emerge."

Nic Pincher

Job: Thief

Tools: Nic seldom needs a tool.
She is so thin, she can get in almost
anywhere. And if there's nowhere
to squeeze through, she can always
follow Rob.

Loves to steal: Anything that glitters
and shines, Theo's socks

Motto: "All that glitters is not gold,
but it's still nice when things are
shiny."

Ellen (Criminellen) Pincher

Job: When Criminellen grows up, she wants to be a thief, just like Rob and Nic.

Tools: Lock pick, slingshot

Loves to steal: Mints, toys

Motto: "Why pay for things when stealing is fun and it's free."

Theo Pincher

Job: When Theo grows up, he wants to be a police officer. (But Rob and Nic don't know that yet.)

Tools: Keys (If he doesn't have keys, he knocks at the door and waits till someone says, "Please come in.")

Loves to steal: Theo doesn't steal. But sometimes he borrows Rob's and Nic's socks without asking.

Motto: "A clean conscience is the best pillow."

Sherlock

Job: Dog (guard dog)

Tools: Sherlock is a dog. He likes barking and pulling on his lead. He doesn't need tools.

Loves to steal: Anything he can eat

Motto: "Woof, Woof, Woof!"
"Shuddup Sherlock! No one understands you anyway!"
"Woof!"

Stola Pincher
(Theo and Ellen's grandma)

Job: Retired thief

Tools: Tiny, sweet cookies (ideally ones you shouldn't eat)

Loves to steal: Anything that glitters and shines (just like Nic)

Motto: "Tittle-tattlers have no friends."

Paul Eessman (lives next to the Pincher family)

Job: Police officer

Tools: Magnifying glass, fingerprint equipment, torch

Loves to steal: NOTHING! GOOD GRIEF, PAUL IS A POLICE OFFICER, POLICE DON'T STEAL, POLICE UN-STEAL!

Motto: "No one turns good from sitting in jail, so it's best to stop the thief before the crime is committed."

IMPORTANT MESSAGE!

Before you read this book: hide your valuables!
Put your phone in your inside pocket.
Keep an eye on your socks. Eat up all your mints!
Don't ever trust the Pincher family.

This story includes:
Disappearing socks
A trip to the toy shop
A watchtower
Strict guards
A great escape
Dynamite
A GOLD DIAMOND!
Action
Love between old people
A happy ending

And remember: if Grandma Pincher
offers you a cookie—DON'T EAT IT!
Got it? Good.
Let's start!

Chapter One

WHO PINCHED THEO'S SOCKS AGAIN?

Every morning when Theo Pincher wakes up, his stripy socks are gone. Every morning this makes him cross.

"Who's pinched my socks?"

Theo's father Rob is at the breakfast table reading the newspaper from next door. He slurps his coffee and wriggles his toes happily. You can only see his toes on one foot, because the other has a sock on it.

"Have you looked under the bed?" he says.

"Of course! There was just an old peppermint stick."
Theo looks at his father's foot. The sock looks very tight.
Like his foot would burst out of it any moment.

"Are you sure you haven't taken my sock?"

His father crosses two fingers behind his back.
"No, no, this is my sock."

Theo's mother Nic is also wearing just one sock.
"It's mine," she says. "I'm absolutely sure. Now, eat
your breakfast and stop talking about socks!"

Theo puts the last slice of bread into the toaster,
the brand-new toaster. His mother came home with
it under her coat one evening last week and since then

Theo's been eating nothing but toast. So has Ellen, his little sister. (Her whole name is Criminellen, but that's hard to say.)

Theo dollops peanut butter onto his toast. Mmm! So good! He's no longer angry. But Ellen is.

"Who took the last piece of toast?" she growls.

"Me." Theo puts the last bit into his mouth. "Sorry, Ellen."

Theo's mother looks at him sternly. "NOW YOU LISTEN HERE, THEO!" she says in capital letters. "I want to hear you saying *NOT* me!"

"But it was me!"

"Doesn't matter. You still say NOT ME. And you cross your fingers behind your back—like this."

"It's called lying," she says. "You have to know how to get anywhere in life."

Theo is good at most things. He can count to a thousand and he's pretty good at drawing. He knows several words in French, and once when the man who lives next door was sick, he helped him by making tea and running to the shop to buy him oranges. Theo is exceptionally good at taking the family's small dog for walks, even though Sherlock is a pain to go out with because he barks so much. Theo is good with dogs because he is very tolerant.

"Shuddup, Sherlock!" says Theo calmly.

"Woof!"

"Mmm, I said, Shuddup, Sherlock!" says Theo, smiling a little.

"WOOF!"

"SHUDDUP, SHERLOCK!"

"WOOOOOF!"

"SHUUUDDUUUP, SHERLOCK!"

But Theo can't lie.

"You must keep trying!" his mother says.

"Do I have to?" Theo asks in a small voice.

She nods seriously.

Now there's someone knocking at the door.

"Open up in the name of the law!" It's Paul Eessman, the man who lives next door. Every morning he comes to get his newspaper back.

Theo's mother looks at him. "You open it," she says. "Tell him the newspaper's not here."

"It is here," whispers Theo, looking at the paper his father's reading.

"Exactly," says Nic. "Tell him it's not and cross your fingers!"

Chapter Two

THEO GETS
A SORE STOMACH

Paul Eessman is wearing a blue cap, a blue jacket with a white strap over the shoulder and an angry frown. But when he sees Theo, his frown disappears. "Good morning, Theo," he says. Theo is a nice boy. He can be trusted. Theo doesn't go around nicking things like the rest of the Pincher family.

Theo never lies.

"Have you seen my newspaper?" asks Paul.

Then he notices that Theo's eyes have gone glassy. "Have you got a stomachache?"

Theo nods. Yes, he has an immense stomachache.

"Have you eaten something bad for you? You have porridge for breakfast, don't you? Very good for the stomach."

Theo shakes his head. "Toast with peanut butter."

"Oh dear." Paul sounds worried. "And I suppose you ate that unhealthy and very expensive peppermint stick I gave you?"

Theo shakes his head. "No, I didn't like it."

Paul smiles stiffly. "I see. Well, have a bowl of proper oat porridge and you'll soon see your stomach come right."

"That's not why I have a sore stomach," says Theo. "It's because Dad took your newspaper."

"In the name of the law! Give me back that paper at once!"

But before his father has time to say sorry, Theo's mother shouts, "Rob bought that newspaper with his own money!"

Paul looks at Theo in surprise.

"But Theo said—"

"He lied," Nic interrupts. "He just lies and lies, that boy."

"I do NOT!" Theo looks almost angry.

"I mean he was joking," she says quickly. "He jokes all the time, that boy."

"Theo? Are you kidding with me?" asks Paul.

"No I'm not!"

Rob slaps Theo on the back. "What do you know?" he sighs. "He's kidding again."

Paul isn't used to kidding and he's not sure how it works. But he doesn't want to look stupid.

"Ha-ha, that was funny." He laughs and pinches Theo's cheek.

"You can borrow my newspaper if you want," says Rob.

Paul shakes his head. "I want MY newspaper. Not yours. Goodbye!"

Chapter Three

THEO'S PARENTS GO TO THE DIAMOND EXHIBITION

Theo has a sore stomach again. He had upset Paul Eessman!

His mother says if Theo had lied properly in the first place, it wouldn't have happened. That's the good thing about lying. If you lie properly, and don't get a sore stomach and glassy eyes all the time, nothing bad will happen.

"But it was Paul Eessman's newspaper," Theo tried.

"And now it's ours," says his mother. "Isn't that right, Rob?"

Rob doesn't answer, he's reading the paper. It looks like he's found something very interesting.

"Can I see?" Nic pinches the newspaper from him and reads it. "Oh, my my!" she mutters.

She takes Rob's last piece of toast and drinks his last slurp of coffee.

"Who would have thought!" she cries.

Then she looks at Theo and Ellen. "Listen, kids, how would you like to sleep all by yourselves for one night?"

Ellen's mouth turns down. "No thanks!"

Ellen is small, and when you're small you want an adult to read you a story, tuck you in and say goodnight when you go to bed.

"Theo can read you a bedtime story."

"I want an adult."

"Theo is practically an adult."

Theo makes himself tall. Yes, he's big now. And not the slightest bit afraid of the dark. As long as he can sleep with the light on.

"You can have ice cream for dinner," says his father.

"And won't have to brush your teeth," says his mother.

Ellen is quiet for a moment.

"Okay then. But where are you going?"

"Look here." Nic holds up the newspaper.

DIAMOND EXHIBITION it says in big letters.

Theo's mother reads:

COME AND SEE
THE FAMOUS GOLD DIAMOND!

The Gold Diamond from the Gold Coast is on
show this weekend in the Gold Room as part
of the diamond exhibition in the Royal
Palace. This weekend, guests who have
purchased a gold ticket will be invited to
a delicious lunch, with the chance to have
a good look at the precious stone.
UP CLOSE!
A warm welcome to all!
Aarti N. Carat, Curator

By the time she's finished reading, Ellen's eyes are
sparkling like diamonds. "I want to come too!"

But Nic shakes her head. There are some things not
suitable for children. That's just how it is.

Underneath what Nic read out is something else in
small letters, but Theo has good eyes.

Den palestinska organisa-
tionen PLO har inte klargjort
     den svenska FN-bataljo-
nen i Sinai för att tillsam-
mans med österrikäre bilda

Se sidan 6

Utförsåkarkungen Inge-
mar Stenmark klarade sig

BURGLARIES UP AROUND COUNTRY

DIAMOND EXHIBITION

Since the Pincher Brothers escaped two days ago, the number of burglaries has increased exponentially.

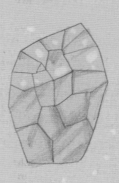

... hardly any crimes solved

Bara 15 procent av brotten klaras upp. 411 poliselever er- sätter 575 behöriga poliser. Ord- ningen på stan ofta dålig. Kni- ven är...bäldet.

Poliskommissarie Nils-Hå- kan Håkansson i Malmö anser att den kampanj som brotts- förebyggande gruppen nu be- drivit i några år börjar ge re- sultat. Malmö är ett av de polisdistrikt som lyckats bäst med att bejda brottsutveck- lingen.

Över hela landet är dock samma utveckling märkbar. Den senaste statistiken över antalet anmälda inbrott visar en minskning med 2,9 proc. för länch...lla, med

The Gold Diamond is on show this weekend in the Gold Room as part of the diamond exhibition in the Royal Palace.

over ersättningar till den ...
...tts- och skattefria sidan ge-
att beteckna belopp som

ungdomsförbundet, sitter i
styrelsen för försvarets ma-
terialverk och är ledamot
i småbusköpskommittén

Warning! Looking but not touching is the
order of the day. Anyone trying to steal
the diamond WILL BE SORRY!

Theo shudders. "Promise you won't pinch the gold diamond?"

"I promise," says his mother, one hand behind her back.

Rob ruffles Theo's hair. "We'll just take a little look," he says. "No touching."

Chapter Four

PAUL EESSMAN WANTS TO GO TO THE DIAMOND EXHIBITION TOO

Together, Nic and Rob pack a bag with everything they need for a diamond exhibition.

They pack:

Rob's biggest crowbar

A good set of pliers

A file

A lock pick

Two false beards

Sunglasses

A small stick of dynamite

They kiss Ellen and Theo and remind them there's ice cream in the freezer, and then Ellen and Theo are on their own.

They play with Sherlock for a while. Theo does the dishes and cleans up the kitchen, and everything feels quite good.

Then Ellen wants to have a look in the toy shop. Theo waits outside while Ellen goes in. Then they both run all the way home.

After they've played again for a while, Ellen wants to go and see if Paul Eessman's apples are as good as they were last year, but Theo thinks it's time for bed.

"Shall we start with the bedtime story?" he asks. "Or would you like ice cream first?"

"Ice cream," says Ellen.

When the ice cream is all gone, Ellen is allowed to choose a story from the big bookshelf in the sitting room. She chooses one filled with small squiggly letters and not a single picture. Now she's lying in bed and Theo is sitting next to her on a chair. Just like an adult.

But it's hard to read like an adult. The book has so many difficult words and strange names.

"...in...the...meantime...Raskolnikov..."

Ellen wriggles impatiently. "Read faster," she says. "Read like a grown-up."

Theo holds the book closer to his face. "In the meantime, Raskolnikov...couldn't..."

Ellen starts crying. "I want a grown-up!" she sobs. "Now!"

· · · · ·

Paul Eessman has just started brushing his teeth when there's a knock at the door. Theo is outside. Ellen stands behind Theo with a book in her arms.

Paul looks at his watch. "Quarter past seven? What are you doing out this late?"

"Can you read Ellen a bedtime story?" Theo asks.

Paul is surprised. "What have you done with your parents?"

"They're out picking flowers," Ellen answers quickly. She's sure it's better if Paul doesn't know they're at a diamond exhibition. He might get the idea that they're up to no good. And then he might want to go and check it out.

Paul scratches his head. Flowers grow in summer. And now it's winter.

"Theo? Is that true?" He looks at Theo with kind but suspicious eyes.

Theo's stomach turns to ice.

"Nyaaah," he mumbles. "It's a bit true…"

But then there is such a squirming in his stomach that he has to rush to tell the whole truth.

"They've gone to the Royal Palace, to the gold diamond exhibition!" He feels better right away.

"Idiot," Ellen whispers to Theo.

"Sorry!" Theo whispers back.

Paul Eessman immediately puts on his jacket and buttons on the white strap. Then he tells Theo to take

Ellen and Sherlock home again. "And don't forget to brush your teeth before you go to bed!"

"Where are you going?" asks Theo.

"I'm going to the Royal Palace! I want to make sure there's no funny business at the diamond exhibition."

Chapter Five

THEO AND ELLEN GO TO JAIL

When they get home, Theo gives Sherlock his dinner. Then he brushes his teeth even though he doesn't have to. Theo likes brushing his teeth. He can't sleep without the taste of toothpaste in his mouth.

Then he sees that Ellen is about to go out.

"I'm going to see Grandma."

"But Grandma's in jail."

"I don't care," says Ellen. "I want an adult."

It's dark outside. Ellen can't go all the way to the jail on her own. Theo goes to get Sherlock's lead.

"I'll come too."

It's only a short walk to the jail. It's a long time past bedtime. There are bars in front of all the jail windows and most of the lights are out. Around the jail is a thick wall topped with barbed wire. There's a gate in the wall and above it a stern sign:

JAIL

Have you broken the law? Welcome!
Otherwise—go away! And don't try any tricks!
Ann Clink, Chief Guard

High up in a glass tower, a guard is scanning the dark with a light, so no one will try any tricks.

"Let's go home again." Theo whispers so the guards won't hear.

But Ellen shrugs off her backpack and pulls out a big slingshot.

"I borrowed it from the toy shop." She scrabbles on the ground till she finds the right-sized stone. "Cover your ears," she says and fires a perfect shot at the tower. The glass shatters with a terrible crunch and the next second, a light shines on Ellen.

"Who did that?" comes a worried voice from above.

"Not me," says Ellen, crossing her fingers behind her back.

"Then it was *you!*" says the voice from above, and now the light shines on Theo.

Theo shakes his head. It certainly wasn't him.

"Really, no? Who WAS it then?"

Theo's stomach hurts. But then the guard catches sight of the slingshot in Ellen's hand.

"Ha, so it was the little girl after all?"

Theo only has to nod the tiniest bit before the gate opens and two overbearing guards rush out to arrest little Ellen.

Theo and Sherlock just manage to sneak in after them before the gate slams shut.

"There," says Ellen. "We're in."

"Woof!"

"Shuddup, Sherlock!"

Ellen and Theo have to follow the guard into a very small room where Ann Clink is squeezed behind a desk, working at a little computer. Every now and then the telephone rings and Ann Clink answers angrily: "Clink, Ann. This is the jail. No, I don't have time! Goodbye!"

She slams down the phone and fastens her gaze on Theo and Ellen. "Names please!"

Ellen stands as tall as she can and says in a high-pitched yet brave voice, "Ellen."

"FULL NAME!"

"Criminellen."

"Suits you," mutters Ann Clink. "And you, pale child? What's your name?"

"Theo," he says in a small voice.

"I can't HEAR you!" thunders Ann Clink. "Your name. First and last names, thank you! No tricks!"

"Oscar Theo Pincher." Theo's voice trembles because he is so scared he has to keep swallowing so as not to cry.

Ann Clink takes a good long look at Theo. "Pincher," she says tightly. "Always these Pinchers. Come on, come and see your grandma."

Chapter Six

LIAR, LIAR, PANTS ON FIRE

Grandma lives down a long corridor with small cell doors along each side. Each cell door has a window you can look through and a solid lock.

"Stola!" calls Ann Clink. "Stola Pincher! You have visitors."

At once, the nearest window opens and a small gangster granny peeps out. "It's after eight!" she hisses. "Shouldn't we have quiet in here by now?"

"Yes, thank you indeed, Popgun," says Ann Clink. "But clearly these little sprouts don't know that."

Theo is ashamed. He's not a sprout. He's a capable boy who brushes his teeth and doesn't lie.

But Ellen looks pleased. "Hi!" she says happily.

"Woof!" says Sherlock.

"Wow, are dogs allowed in here now?" mutters Popgun. "Imagine if I was ALLERGIC?"

She suddenly looks sly. "Want to know a secret?"

Yes, Ann Clink would love to.

"Stola isn't in her cell like she should be. She and Cheater-Rita snuck out a while ago. I think they ran down to the gym. Are they allowed to?"

Ann Clink shakes her head. "No, they absolutely are not!"

A gym is where you go to train your muscles. You can do weightlifting or bike very fast on a training cycle. At the gym, Grandma is doing chin-ups. Another gangster granny is cheering her on.

"Come on, Stola! You can do better than that. One more! Come on!"

"Shut up," puffs Grandma. "How many have I done?"

"Three."

Grandma lies with her face on the floor.

"That's enough for tonight," she sighs. "Your turn, Cheater-Rita!"

Cheater-Rita throws herself to the floor.

"One, two, three, six, nine, thirteen, twenty! Done. I did thirty."

She lies with her face to the floor just like Grandma, catching her breath. Then she sees Theo. "Who's this little fart?" she giggles.

Grandma turns around and whoops in delight.

"But DARLINGS! I'm so HAPPY to see you!"

Theo and Ellen each receive a long hard hug. But then Grandma has to go nicely back to her cell.

Because Ellen broke a window, Ann Clink says it would do her good to stay a night in jail and think about what she's done. And since Theo and Sherlock

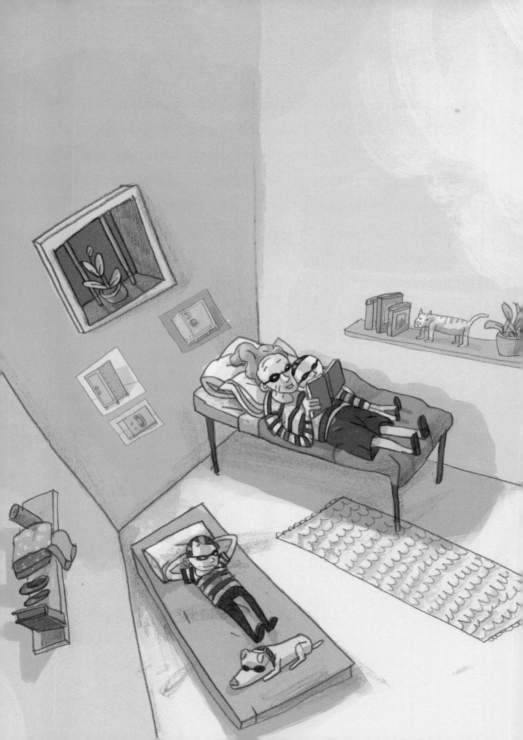

can't manage on their own, she goes off to fetch an extra mattress. But it will only be for one night, because children are not actually allowed in jail.

Unfair, thinks Ellen. When she grows up, she'll change that.

Sherlock is soon asleep at Theo's feet and Grandma is reading a goodnight story. Every time she finishes a chapter, Ellen shouts, "More! Just ONE more? Please Grandma!"

After an hour someone knocks on the wall. "Are you allowed to read out loud this late?" says a cross voice.

"You are if your GRANDCHILDREN are visiting!"

"Dirty donkey," comes the voice through the wall. "If you don't stop yakking with your grandkids, I'll tell the guards on you."

Grandma looks at Theo and Ellen. "Take no notice of Popgun Gail," she sighs. "She's just jealous."

"I am NOT," comes through the wall.

Grandma yawns and puts the book aside. She's almost asleep already. But then she opens an eye. "Hey, you two. What have you done with Nic and Rob?"

Theo glances at Ellen. "Can we tell Grandma?"

Ellen nods. They absolutely can tell Grandma. Theo explains that his father and mother have gone to the diamond exhibition in the Royal Palace, so they can look at the fantastically large gold diamond.

"But they're just looking," says Theo, "not touching."

Grandma has come wide awake in a second. "Did you say gold diamond?"

Then she whispers, quietly so Popgun Gail won't hear: "What say we run away?"

Chapter Seven

THE GREAT ESCAPE

The difficult thing about running away from jail is that the door's locked from the outside. But Grandma has a lock pick, for picking locks.

Another difficult thing is the guards, all sneaking around the prison, keeping an eye on things. But Grandma takes out a flat tin with beautiful summer clouds on the lid. Inside are a whole lot of little, round golden-yellow cookies with pink-sugared edges.

"These cookies make people nice," says Grandma. She smiles cunningly.

"Can I try?" Ellen snatches one.

"Nix pix." Grandma takes the cookie from Ellen. "They're for guards only."

"Not fair," mumbles Ellen. "When I'm big I'll—"

"Shhh!" Grandma has picked the lock to her cell. She opens the door carefully and peeps out. There's just one night lamp shining in the corridor and sounds of snoring from the cells.

"Cheater-Rita will want to come too," whispers Grandma. "Wait here!"

Theo and Ellen stand nervously outside Grandma's cell.

"Hurry up!" calls Ellen.

At once, Popgun Gail's cell door opens.

"What's this? Are you running away?" she says when she sees the children.

"Yes," says Theo. Then, "Ow!" when Ellen kicks him in the shin.

But it's already too late.

"Stola's running away!" Popgun yells. "Guards! Stola Pincher's on the run!"

"She's not," hisses Ellen, but Popgun takes no notice.

"Escape! Hello! Someone here's getting away!"

And now a guard comes running and glaring.

"What's going on here?" she cries, waving her baton.

Theo is so scared he almost forgets to breathe. But then he remembers Grandma's cookies. Which make you nice. The guard could sure do with one.

"Do you want to taste something really good?" Theo takes the lid off the tin.

The guard goes into raptures. Suddenly, she doesn't look at all angry.

"Are there raisins?"

"I don't think so," says Theo.

"I've actually brushed my teeth already," says the guard. "But one cookie won't hurt. Or maybe two."

So, she takes two and pops them into her mouth. She smiles and smacks her lips.

"They're delicious."

Then the guard sinks gently to the floor, curls up like a little cat and falls fast asleep.

Theo's eyes are wide. Grandma has put SLEEPING TABLETS in the cookies. The guard looks to be having a very good sleep. Theo gets a quilt from Grandma's bed and slips a pillow under her head, so her neck won't hurt when she wakes.

And now Grandma has picked the lock to Cheater-Rita's cell. Cheater-Rita hops right out and gives Grandma a happy slap on the back.

"This'll be fun!" she chuckles.

"Unfair!" calls Popgun Gail. "I want to run away too."

Chapter Eight

PAUL EESSMAN
GETS A COOKIE

By the time Grandma, Ellen, Theo and Cheater-Rita are finally on the street outside the jail, there aren't many cookies left in the tin. The guards are sleeping soundly, every one of them, all with smiles on their faces.

Grandma looks around for a getaway vehicle. She spies an old car rusting beneath a tree.

"We'll take that old banger!" she cries, taking out her lock pick.

But this is too much for Theo. You can't break windows in watchtowers. You can't bake cookies that

make people fall asleep. And you absolutely can't steal other people's cars.

"You can leave that alone!" But it's not Theo shouting, it's Cheater-Rita. "That's my car. And it's not a banger."

Grandma backs away from the car.

"I parked it here before I went to jail," Cheater-Rita mutters. She starts brushing away the leaves. "She looks terrible!" Cheater-Rita takes a piece of paper from under a windscreen wiper. "A parking ticket too, wouldn't that rip your knickers."

She fishes a key from her trouser pocket and opens the door.

"Hop in!"

Theo and Ellen crawl under a blanket on the back seat. Ellen is already yawning and Theo's eyes are heavy. By the time the car starts rolling, both children are fast asleep.

"Jump up, Pincher-kids!" In no time, Grandma is gently shaking them awake. "We're here!"

It's the middle of the night. Outside the car is a large and beautiful building. The roof gleams through the darkness and an ostentatious sign hangs over the entrance:

DIAMOND EXHIBITION

Sherlock starts barking madly and pawing at the back door. "Shuddup, Sherlock!" Theo whispers, but Sherlock doesn't stop.

Outside the diamond exhibition is a lanky figure, prowling and snooping about. He has blue clothing, a police cap and a white strap over his shoulder.

It's Paul Eessman.

"Duck!" hisses Grandma, rolling into a ball on the front seat. Ellen and Theo huddle together in the back and Theo puts his hand over Sherlock's muzzle. But Cheater-Rita just sits there, looking at Paul Eessman, her eyes glistening like gold diamonds.

"What are you glistening for?" Grandma whispers irritably.

"See for yourself how cute he is," Cheater-Rita sighs. "How adorable he looks, sneaking around like that."

"That bucket-head is always turning up, sticking his nose where it's not wanted. What's he doing now?"

"He's found a hole in the wall, I think. It looks like someone set off a little stick of dynamite."

Theo sits up. What if it was his parents' little stick of dynamite?

Oh! Theo suddenly feels how badly he's missing them. He wants them to come out through that little hole right now. They should forget about the stupid gold diamond and worry about him and Ellen instead. They should all go home. Then they could make tea and turn on the kitchen radio and say: "Time for bed now, sweet peas!"

Paul is crouched in front of the hole. But just as he sticks his head in, Sherlock manages to open the car door.

"Woof!"

First Paul looks alarmed, but when he sees it's Sherlock, he grins. "Well, old boy, what are you doing here?"

Then he catches sight of Cheater-Rita's car.

"I recognize that old banger."

Paul Eessman never forgets a car. He's sure he stuck a ticket on this very one, not so long ago. Outside Ann Clink's jail. He remembers it well. But what's it doing here? Is there something funny going on?

Inside the car, Grandma hisses crossly at Cheater-

Rita to drive closer. She opens her tin and takes out one of the last cookies. She winds down the window and aims carefully at Paul Eessman's mouth.

"Wait!" whispers Ellen, handing over her slingshot. "This is better."

Now Paul is closer than ever to the car.

Theo is still lying down on the back seat, his heart thumping.

Grandma places the cookie in the sling and pulls it back. She takes aim and fires. A perfect shot. Right into Paul Eessman's mouth.

"Hmmph! What is this wonderful thing in my mouth?" says Paul in surprise, and he swallows the cookie.

Then he yawns and rolls onto the ground. Soon he is snoring quietly, a smile on his face.

Chapter Nine

HERE COME THE POLICE!

Cheater-Rita can't stop looking at Paul.

"He's so gorgeous," she says.

"Pull yourself together!" says Grandma. "That guy's a policeman so you can never trust him. COME ON!"

Theo wants to tell Grandma she's wrong about Paul. You absolutely can trust him. It's Grandma who's putting sleeping pills in cookies and escaping from jail all the time. Not Paul Eessman. But before he can say anything, Grandma has crept in through the hole in the wall. And now Ellen and Cheater-Rita are crawling after her.

Theo takes the blanket from the car and lays it over Paul.

"Sleep well!" he whispers before he too crawls in through the hole.

TO THE
GOLD DIAMOND

Inside the hole is a long corridor with no lights. Just the sound of happy voices in the distance, as if there's a party happening a very long way away.

Grandma takes Theo by the hand.

"Shhh! Not a peep! And stop trembling!"

Theo is scared. He's never been so scared in all his life.

Cheater-Rita has found a stairwell with a sign: TO THE GOLD DIAMOND

"Shhh!" hushes Grandma with a warning finger to her lips.

Everyone is quiet, even Sherlock.

"Shush!" Grandma says again.

"We are shushing!" Cheater-Rita snorts.

"I said SSHHH!" hisses Grandma, not so quiet now, more angry.

"HHSSHH YOURSELF!" whispers Cheater-Rita, with a finger to her own lips.

58

Grandma and Cheater-Rita stop a minute, each with a finger to their lips, saying Shhh! to each other. Ssshhh! Sssshhh! Shush thief!

"Okay," whispers Grandma at last. "Up the stairs!"

Grandma goes first, then Cheater-Rita, then Theo, Ellen and Sherlock.

At the top there's a door. Grandma carefully places her hand on the handle. Before opening, she turns to Cheater-Rita.

"We go halves, right?"

"Of course," says Cheater-Rita.

But Theo sees that she's kept her hand behind her back. And that her fingers are crossed.

The gold diamond is lying on a large velvet cushion in the middle of the gold room. It's the biggest diamond Theo's ever seen. There are no lights on, but still the room is bathed in light.

"Last one there's a goody gumdrop!" cries Cheater-Rita.

But Grandma holds her back.

There are two people in the gold room already. Wearing striped clothing. With beards and sunglasses.

Theo knows the beards. They're the ones his parents had packed before they left.

But what are they doing?

His parents had promised Theo they'd only look at the diamond! No touching! Why does his father have that crowbar? And why is his mother looking around so furtively?

"Oh! They're pinching the gold diamond," whispers Grandma. "Right in front of our eyes."

Theo watches as his father raises the crowbar, ready to wallop it down. His mother looks at him. She gives him an excited nod, as if she's saying, "Go on! Smash it!"

"STOP! POLICE!"

Theo's father stops. He looks around.

"What?"

"THE POLICE ARE COMING!"

"Theo?"

And Theo runs over to his parents. He shouts louder than he's ever shouted before.

"POLIIIICE!"

Chapter Ten

THEO STARTS TO CRY

The whole gang of thieves tumbles out through the door and down the stairs. They run, fast as they can, along the corridor, through the hole in the wall. They scramble past Paul Eessman, still asleep, and crouch behind Cheater-Rita's car.

And now there's a hugging party.

Theo expects his mother and his father to be angry with him and Ellen for turning up in the middle of the night. But Nic is just pleased that Theo warned them about the police in time.

"You are such a good boy." She hugs Theo several times over.

"Thank you," whispers Theo.

Grandma looks around. "Has anyone seen Cheater-Rita?" She sounds worried.

Cheater-Rita is nowhere to be seen.

"What if the police've got her?" says Ellen anxiously.

"They probably haven't," says Theo.

"What makes you say that?" Ellen asks.

Theo looks weakly at Ellen. And at Grandma. "Because …because…she's here!" he says, as Cheater-Rita spills out through the hole in the wall.

"Quick!" she cries. "The police are after me—at least a hundred! Time to split!" But she ducks down beside the sleeping Paul Eessman and gives him a quick kiss on the cheek. "Seeya, gorgeous!"

"Bye, sweet peas!" says Grandma, with an extra-loving look at Theo. "You were so clever to warn us in time," she says. "We'll make a fine thief of you yet."

And she hops into Cheater-Rita's car.

"Bye, Grandma!" calls Ellen. But the car has already skidded around the corner, out of sight.

Theo's mother yawns. "We should probably go home too." Then she looks around.

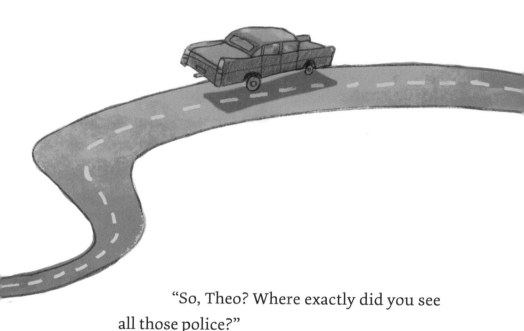

"So, Theo? Where exactly did you see all those police?"

Theo feels his stomach turn to ice. He can't answer because suddenly a whole flood of tears is banking up inside him.

His father lifts him up and holds him close.

"The boy's crying," he whispers in surprise to Nic and Ellen. "What's this about?" he asks Theo.

Theo whispers back. But he's whispering into his father's shoulder so the words are muffled.

"What did you say?"

Theo turns his head and looks red-eyed at his mother. "I lied," he sniffs. "I liiiiiiiied!"

"Do you mean to say..."

"There were no police. I made it up..."

First his mother looks angry. Her eyes go small, and her mouth tightens. But then the anger melts from her eyes and her mouth turns soft and happy again. She comes over and strokes Theo on the back.

"You were a good boy," she says lovingly. "At long last, my little boy's learned to lie!"

Then Theo's father lifts Paul Eessman up and carries him in his strong arms over to the Pincher family's dented car. He puts Paul in the back since he's still sound asleep. Theo gets to sit on his mother's lap, and all the way home she keeps patting him on the head and telling him he's the best boy in the whole world.

To think he's finally learned to lie. Like a genuine Pincher!

Chapter Eleven

PAUL EESSMAN GETS A LETTER

But Theo's not ready to stop telling the truth. The very next morning when Paul Eessman turns up wondering who's taken his newspaper, Theo points at Rob.

"Him!"

But Rob has just found a very interesting article. It's about someone blowing a hole in the Royal Palace with a little stick of dynamite and the gold diamond vanishing without trace.

"Theo's kidding you," he mutters to Paul.

Paul Eessman laughs awkwardly. And when he wonders aloud how he could have woken in his own bed this morning, when the last thing he remembers is going through a hole in a wall, Theo tells him exactly what happened. "Grandma flicked a sleeping cookie into your mouth," he says.

"You're kidding," Paul Eessman laughs. "You think you can trick me, you little rascal."

A few days later Paul comes to the Pincher family's door. But he doesn't yell: "Open in the name of the law and hand over my newspaper!" He doesn't even knock. Just taps, three soft taps.

Theo opens the door. "We have your newspaper if you're wondering," he says.

"Uff! I don't care about an old newspaper."

Paul leans against the doorpost and sighs. "Do you know what, Theo? I think I'm in love."

"Congratulations!" says Theo. "Who with?"

Paul looks a little worried. "Well, that's just it. I don't know exactly. But her name's Rita. And she has very neat handwriting."

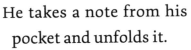

He takes a note from his pocket and unfolds it.

"Dear handsome Paul Eessman," he reads. "Here is a gift from me that shines as bright as your twinkly blue eyes. A thousand kisses from your eternal admirer. Cheater-Rita."

"She gave me this."

Paul Eessman hunts under his shirt.

"Look! A lovely necklace."

The necklace itself isn't so special. Just your average chain. But on the chain hangs a jewel. A diamond. The biggest diamond Theo has ever seen. But no, he has seen it before. It glowed just as brightly that time too.

"It's very nice, isn't it?" Paul sighs again.

"Very nice!"

"Do you think it would have been incredibly expensive?" Paul wonders.

"I'm sure it was," says Theo.

"Woof!"

"Shuddup, Sherlock!"

THE END

UP NEXT

and the Dog Chase

THE EXCITING NEXT BOOK ABOUT
THE PINCHER FAMILY INCLUDES:

Talking dogs

A bad police officer

A candy store robbery

Police interrogation

Surprising news

A super-smart plan

Clampdown

Action

Mister Christer

Chapter One

HEY THERE, BUDDY!

Remember me? Of course you do!

I'm the dog in this family. I've been the family dog for as long as I can remember. All my life maybe. Several years anyway. Or is it months? My memory's not great.

I like my family! The food is good and they're kind to me. The mother can get angry, though. Usually with the boy, because he's really bad at crossing his fingers behind his back.

The girl keeps her fingers crossed the whole time. This makes the mother happy, so she shows all her teeth and pats the girl's hair. Then she looks at the boy and points at the girl and says something with her strange words. Then the boy is sad.

We dogs notice things like that.

I don't know exactly what the mother says. People are no good at talking in a way that dogs can understand. But I know what my name is because the family use it all time. And when I hear it, I wag my tail and answer happily.

"Hi! Hello! Here I am! Snack time? Hello? Hi! D'you hear me? Dinner, dinner, dinner time?"

Then they use my name again. "Sherlock!" they yell. "Shuddup Sherlock!"

Shuddup Sherlock, that's me.

Nice name, don't y'think?

READ MORE IN *The Pinchers and the Dog Chase*

Discover your inner Pincher and turn
the page for criminal activities!

Learn your thief name, find out
what kind of thief you are, train
your criminal mind, and test
your Pincher knowledge.

Find your criminal name!

Use our name generator to find your criminal name.

1. Your criminal first name comes from
    the first letter in your name.

Apple	Kitty	Underhand
Badluck	Lurka	Vessel
Cat	M. Bezzle	Weasel
Dee Vius	Nestegg	X-con
Emerald	Obstacle	Y-mee
Fortune	Polite	Zircon
Goldie	Quartz	
Honest	Ransom	
Illgreen	Shifty	
Jules	Trixie	

2. Your criminal surname comes from
   the month you were born.

   January: Swindle
   February: Pilfer
   March: Scammer
   April: Purloin
   May: Stickemups
   June: Robberson
   July: Take-it
   August: Looter
   September: Pickets
   October: Snatch
   November: Sneakers
   December: Nickett

Your partner in crime

Many thieves have pets, especially dogs, goldfish or dust rats! Use our name generator to find the criminal name of your partner in crime.

Your pet's criminal name comes from the continent you live on.

Antarctica: Dynamite

Oceania: Bling

Asia: Crystal

Africa: Dent

South America: Spit

North America: Ninja

Europe: Sir Valence

Quiz: What kind of thief are you?

1. When you come to a closed door, how do you get in?

    A. With a crowbar
    B. With a lock pick
    C. With a small stick of dynamite
    D. You knock

2. It's time to rob the museum!
   How will you plan?

   A. Check where the surveillance cameras are located
   B. Study the drawings carefully
   C. Plan? Let's just get it done!
   D. Pay the entrance fee and look at the exhibition

3. What are you wearing on your head?

   A. Villain mask
   B. Fedora
   C. Earmuffs
   D. A beanie (if it's winter)

4. What is the most important thing about a heist?

   A. Getting away with the booty
   B. Solving a really tricky problem
   C. Blowing something up
   D. That no one gets scared or injured or loses anything

5. Do you have an accomplice?

   A. My partner and I do everything together
   B. I work with a code-cracking robot
   C. I work on my own—but always with my tiger, of course
   D. Sometimes I bring a classmate or cousin

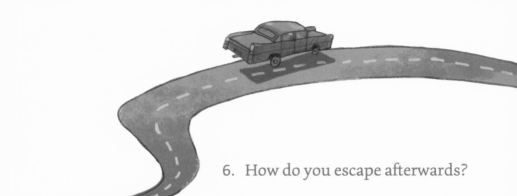

6. How do you escape afterwards?

A. Pinch a bike and pedal away
B. My accomplice is ready,
   as planned, with a getaway car
C. In my space rocket
D. I phone in to report myself to
   the police

7. What is your dream place to rob?

A. Somewhere packed with gold bars
B. Shops full of things that sparkle and glitter
C. A fireworks factory
D. The recycling facility so I can help
   categorize all the things that
   weren't sorted correctly

8. How do you celebrate a successful heist?

   A. Candy buffet
   B. Juice and cake
   C. A thunderous fireworks display
   D. Sharing with others

Count how many of each letter
you got then turn the page
to reveal your thief type.

Mostly A
THIEVING THIEF

You can't plan forever; sometimes you have to act. You've seen a lot of villain movies and know classic tricks like disguise, evasion and effective withholding of the truth. You're an expert with lock pick, crowbar and other tools.
Nothing stops you!

Mostly B
OLD-SCHOOL THIEF

You are prepared to put in a lot of time thinking and like to study plans day and night. Preparation is key! Who has time to sit in jail? The impossible is a challenge for you. After every successful heist you skip away unnoticed.

Mostly C
EXTRA EVERYTHING THIEF

Extravagance is your watchword.
Life is for living, and for you that means
dynamite, fireworks and robberies with extra
everything. Not everyone dares or wants to do
what you do, but one thing is for sure—
everyone will know where you've been.

Mostly D
HONORABLE THIEF

You are honest and stand by that. Things can
go wrong, of course—you might think it's
okay to take the last potato even though a hungry
dinner companion misses out. But you would
never knowingly break the law, and you don't
like to make others sad.

Did you get a mix
of letters? Then you are
a combination of thief types!
That's often how it is:
you're a little this and
a little that.

Quiz: How well do you know the Pincher family?

1. What is Ellen's real name?

   A. Criminellen

   B. Chanterelle

   C. Caramel

2. Where does Grandma Stola Pincher live?

   A. A castle

   B. A hotel

   C. Jail

3. What happens if you eat Grandma Stola's cookies?

   A. You get full

   B. You blush

   C. You fall asleep

4. How does Theo's body feel when he lies?

   A. His teeth start to grind

   B. He wants to sneeze

   C. His stomach hurts

5. How do you get a Pincher to tell the truth?

   A. Point out their nervous twitching

   B. Force them to show all ten fingers

   C. Tickle their stomachs

6. What do the Pinchers steal from Paul Eessman?

   A. His socks

   B. His morning paper

   C. His uniform

7. You know Paul Eessman's job—but do you know how to spell it (mostly)?

   A. Police

   B. Pollees

   C. Polliiiiiicccce!

You'll find the answers on page 97.
How many did you get right?

Train your criminal mind!

The Pincher family likes to take things that aren't theirs. Sometimes thieving requires a really good memory, so it's time for memory training.

Look carefully at the picture below and try to memorize every object. When you're done, turn the page and see how much you can remember!

Tip!
Look at the picture
for a full minute.

Can you answer these questions about the picture?

1. There are two paintings. What do they depict?

2. What shape is the road sign?

3. Was there anything suitable for winter sports? What was that?

4. How many apples did you find?

5. Was the stuffed lion wearing glasses?

6. How many wheels did you see?

7. Did you see anything belonging to Paul Eessman?

8. Now see if you can write down everything you saw!

Answers to Pincher family quiz: 1a, 2c, 3c, 4c, 5b, 6b, 7a

Answers to questions opposite:

1. A royal person (in a crown) and a ship at sea   2. Triangle   3. Ski boots

4. 29   5. There was no stuffed lion! The bear was not wearing glasses.

6. 4   7. A baton

Where is the
picture that
should be
here?

THief!!

If you've taken
the picture
you must put
it back
IMMEDIATELY!!

Sincerely
Per and Anders